# Mal's DIARY

Disney PRESS

Los Angeles • New York

Printed in China
First Edition, July 2015
1 3 5 7 9 10 8 6 4 2
F383-2370-2-15107
Library of Congress Control Number: 2014960190
ISBN 978-1-4847-2685-3

For more Disney Press fun, visit www.disneybooks.com
Visit DisneyDescendants.com

DISNEY

# Mal's DIARY

Adapted by TINA McLEEF

Based on the film created and written by

JOSANN McGIBBON & SARA PARRIOTT

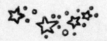

DISNEP PRESS

Los Angeles • New York

They say I'm trouble
THEY SAY I'M BAD
They say I'm evil
THAT MAKES ME GLAD

I'm from the Isle of the Lost. It's the place that people from Auradon know as That Island Across the Way, the one where all the villains and their children were banished to. I like that the streets are dirty, and the windows of every building are broken, and the storefronts are boarded up. It's a place where evil lurks, where apples are poisoned and dark spells are cast. But for me and my friends?

## IT'S HOME SWEET HOME

I DON'T REMEMBER ANYTHING ELSE BESIDES THIS LIFE. IT'S JUST ME AND MOM—KNOWN AS MALEFICENT—ONE OF THE MOST EVIL VILLAINS IN THE WORLD.

I'm ROTTEN to the core
Who could ask for more
I'M NOTHING LIKE
the kid next door

She cast a spell on Aurora, aka Sleeping Beauty, years ago, and apparently people are still pretty angry about it (those goody-two-shoes princesses really know how to hold a grudge). But Mom doesn't care, and neither do I. **We're happy here. Or the villain equivalent of "happy." "Content in our evilness"??**

# I SPEND MOST OF MY TIME WITH MY FRIEND JAY.

I've also been hanging out with Carlos and Evie. Jay is Jafar's son. Jafar went after Aladdin, some street kid, a few years back, and it was a bad scene. Carlos's mom is Cruella De Vil (big white hair, ugly red boots, a fake Dalmatian coat that she always talks to . . . you can't miss her). And Evie? When we first met we didn't really get along, but as I got to know her better, that changed. She's the Evil Queen's daughter, and besides being a little obsessed with her magic mirror (and boys . . . ugh), she's pretty cool. Anyway, the four of us know how to kill time like nobody's business. We've tagged the walls of every shop on the island. We like to run through the market, terrorizing kids, kicking over trash cans, and playing Who's the Scariest of Them All? Jay's stolen from almost everyone who lives here. He's got more booty than Evie's mom.

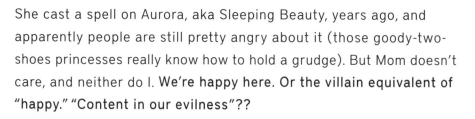

IT'S A WICKED, WILD LIFE. I'M LEARNING TO BE EVIL, JUST LIKE MY MOM IS, JUST LIKE SHE WANTS ME TO BE.

they couldn't stand the SIGHT of us

She was the one who told me about the king, Beast. He and his wife, Belle, sent all of us villains here because they couldn't stand the sight of us. Heaven forbid everyone on Auradon isn't all cheery, sugary-sweet goodness. Now that place is overrun with young princes and princesses, with stuck-up, snobby citizens who think they're better than everyone else, especially us villains. Mom is just waiting for her chance at revenge, and I promised her I'll be ready when she strikes back.

IF SHE'S THE MOST EVIL VILLAIN IN THE LAND, I NEED TO BE THE SECOND MOST EVIL VILLAIN IN THE LAND. LIKE MOTHER, LIKE DAUGHTER, RIGHT?

MIRROR MIRROR on THE WALL who's the BADDEST of them all? welcome to my WICKED world

Mom caught me in the market today, snatching candy from a baby. You would've thought she'd have been thrilled, but she kept going on and on about how I was thinking "small" and how being mean is different from being evil. She lectured me in front of all of my friends. It was kind of humiliating. Then, if that wasn't enough, she told us we're all being sent to a new school—Auradon Prep.

# WHAT THE????!?!?

Yes. Auradon Prep. It's the boarding school in Auradon filled with preppy, proper princesses and princes and other kids who think just like them. **Auradon Prep.** Known for its flowers and rainbows and cheer. There's no way we're going. It doesn't matter how much my mom wants us to. Carlos is terrified of dogs (and apparently Auradon has a ton), and Jay wouldn't be caught dead in a school uniform. Evie's the only one who's excited, but that's just because she wants to meet a prince, fall in love, become a legit princess, blah blah blah blah. The one thing she doesn't realize: if we go there, we'll be outcasts. Everyone in Auradon hates our parents. No one will want to look at us, let alone be friends with us. I don't know where this decision came from, but we're supposed to go talk to my mom and find out. She mentioned something about the king's son, Ben, and "seeking world domination." **More on that later. . . .**

**SO APPARENTLY MY MOM HAS A PLAN.** No surprise there—she always does. But this one is a little different. It's been twenty years since my mom was banished to the Isle of the Lost, and her magic doesn't work like it used to. She can't use her spell book to conjure love spells or send princesses into dark, dreamless sleeps for decades. She can't even grow a forest full of thorns. On the Isle of the Lost her powers are weakened,

# BUT ALL THAT COULD CHANGE....

# ENTER ME AND MY FRIENDS.

**SINCE, FOR SOME REASON, WE'VE BEEN INVITED** to attend Auradon Prep, we will be on, duh, Auradon, a place where my mom's spell book actually works. She wants us to go there and steal the Fairy Godmother's wand, so she can have both the wand and her scepter, which will allow her to bend both good and evil to her will. ✶ ✶ ✶ ✶ ✶ ✶ ✶ ✶ ✶ ✶ ✶ ✶ ✶ ✶ ✶

# THE EVIL QUEEN EVEN AGREED TO GIVE US HER MAGIC MIRROR,

which would help us figure out where the wand is as soon as we get there. Once we find the wand and return it to my mom, the spell will be broken. All the villains from the Isle of the Lost will return to the good ol' US of A, where we'll wreak havoc once again. No more rules. No more listening to the Beast, who isn't even *our* king. No more imprisonment here, on this island.

Nothing will be able to stop us if we have that wand.

## HERS AND HERS CROWNS. THAT WAS WHAT MY MOM PROMISED ME.

That we'll rule together. She swears this isn't just about her, that she wants me to learn all of her evil ways, that I can have the same power she does. But why does it always *feel* like it's about her? Like she's using me to get what she wants? **If you refuse,** she'd said, **you're grounded for the rest of your life.** There goes my say in the matter. **There goes MY CHOICE.**

*It was like she didn't even care...*

*For once, I just want her to stop and do something NORMAL. Ordinary.*

Like, instead of going on and on about world domination, maybe she could just, like . . . take me somewhere fun. Or talk to me about normal stuff, like what I think about the Isle of the Lost, or what I do with my friends when she's home all day, plotting. And how come none of my friends' parents were quite as eager to just ship their kids off to some ridiculous boarding school? **It was like she didn't even care . . . like she wouldn't even miss me.**

# HOW TO BE EVIL
## AKA LESSONS FROM MOM
-----------------------------------------

*She has actually tried to teach me a few things, so maybe she does care.*

- **DON'T sweat the small stuff. There's a difference between being mean and being truly evil.**
- Always think BIG: seek world domination, curse entire kingdoms, cast spells on kings and queens.
- **DO UNTO OTHERS AS THEY DO TO YOU.**
- Don't let people mistreat you.
- **Rude, crude people must be punished. Always SEEK REVENGE.**
- To receive an invitation to an important event is an act of courtesy and respect. If you have been DENIED an invite to something important, SEEK REVENGE.
- **YOU MUST BE LOATHED AND FEARED.**
- Never get attached. **TO ANYONE. EVER.**
- **NEVER FALL IN LOVE. It makes you weak and you may lose everything.**
- Spells for all reasons and seasons. Anything you need can be conjured. Manipulation, power, and influence all come from spells.
- **ALWAYS CONSULT YOUR SPELL BOOK.**
- Look good. Wrap your horns in python skin and bat hides. Make sure your cape is ironed and your scepter is polished at all times.
- A little powder goes a long way. Always accentuate your cheekbones.

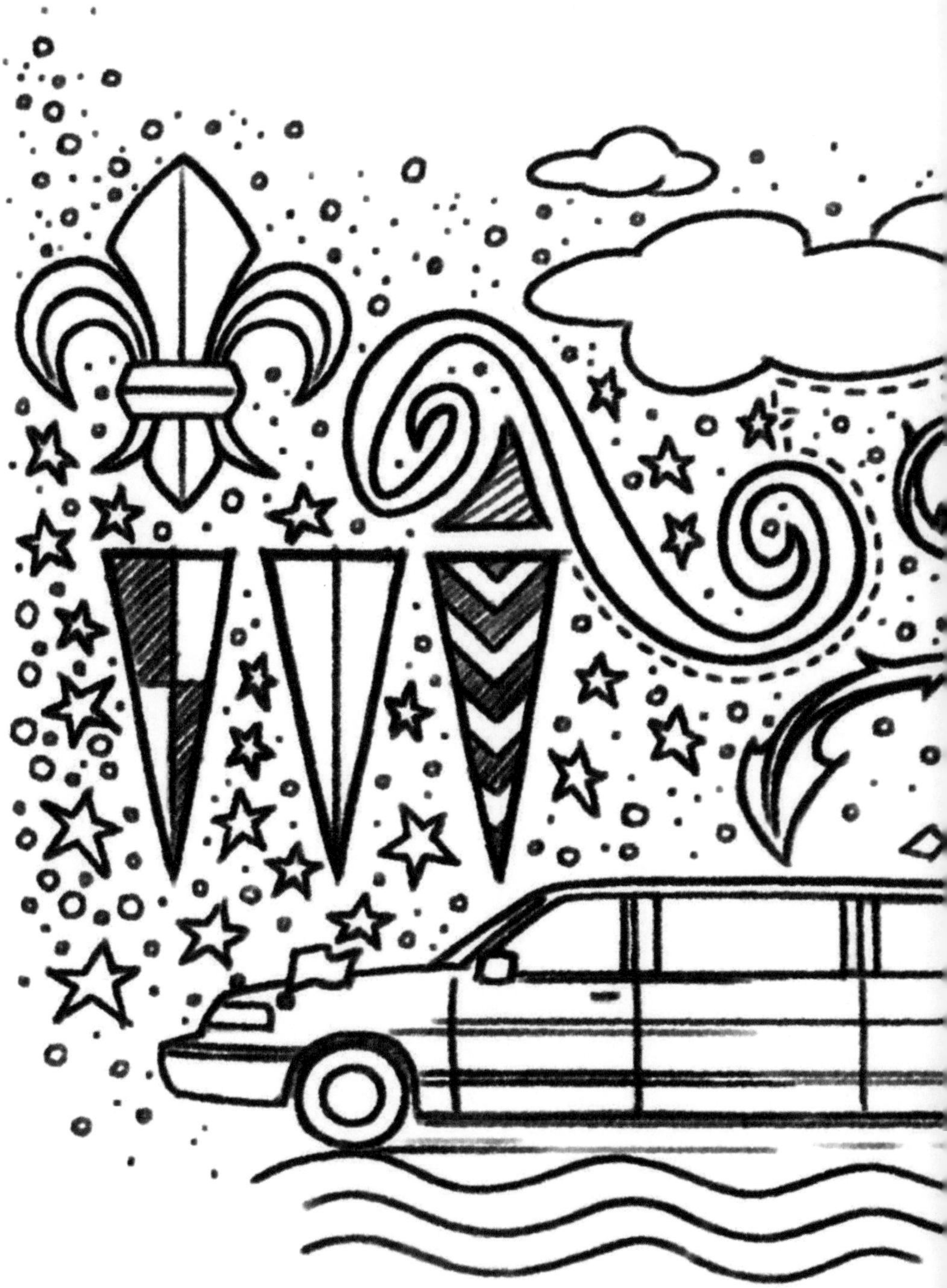

# I'M WRITING THIS FROM A STRETCH LIMO.

At least they're bringing us to Auradon Prep in style. They sent the car early this morning, and when Jay, Carlos, Evie, and I climbed in, we couldn't believe it. It's stocked with every type of candy—peanut butter cups, chocolate-covered pretzels, gummi bears—and has this crazy sound system that Jay's already dismantled (of course). He's stealing the speakers and hood ornament, too, because, hey! What better way to say "We're villains and you were stupid to invite us into your school!" than with petty theft?

## THE LIMO JUST BROKE THE BARRIER INTO AURADON. A MAGIC BRIDGE APPEARED AND LET US CROSS BACK ONTO THE MAINLAND FROM THE ISLE OF THE LOST.

It was pretty cool, I have to admit, seeing the bridge appear out of nowhere. They say it'll still be a little while until we get there. Carlos has been staring out the window, looking to see if Auradon is filled with wild dogs like his mom said. Jay's playing with his new electronics, and Evie is nervously reapplying her makeup. At one point, she asked me what I was thinking about. I said I was plotting (an easy excuse), but it was really more than that. I can't stop thinking about yesterday and how our parents were treating us. Carlos is practically his mom's slave, fluffing her furs and scraping the bunions from her feet. Jay has to work for his dad in the shop, and poor Evie always has the Evil Queen whispering in her ear, telling her she needs to find a prince to marry, as if that's the most important thing in the world.

Maybe Auradon Prep, as proper and good (ick, I hate that word) as it is, will be a nice (I hate that word, too) break from the Isle of the Lost. Maybe it won't just be a chance for world domination. Maybe it'll be a chance for us to get away for a week or two . . . like a little vacation from our parents.

## I MEAN, NOT EVERYONE THERE CAN BE PRIM AND PROPER AND AWFUL, CAN THEY?

And even if they are, a change of scenery might not hurt. I've been on that island for sixteen years now, walking the same streets every day. I could tell you the name of every shopkeeper, every kid who cuts school, every guy Jay's ever sold stolen electronics to. Every day Evie, Jay, Carlos, and I do the same thing—go out, cause some trouble, come home. It doesn't even feel exciting anymore. Maybe Auradon Prep will be exciting. I mean, a limo ride over an invisible bridge is already more exciting than my last ten days on the island combined. Maybe there'll be more things like this . . . more things to look forward to.

OR MAYBE IT'LL BE TERRIBLE, AND WE'LL ALL BE OUTCASTS. BUT A GIRL CAN DRE*AM,

*CAN'T SHE?

So apparently this whole Save the Children thing was Prince Ben's idea. He's the Beast and Beauty's son, and he's inheriting the crown, which I guess makes him a soon-to-be king. We stepped out of the limo and he was all: "I hope this day will go down in history as the day our two peoples began to heal." How's that for dumb optimism?

I WANTED TO ROLL MY EYES/GAG BUT I HAD TO PRETEND WE WERE HAPPY TO BE THERE.

# HE ACTUALLY WANTS TO GIVE US, THE CHILDREN OF THE VILLAINS,

a chance at a normal life. To give us the choice between good and evil. I hate to be the one to break it to him, but we're our parents' kids. We've been stealing, lying, and cheating since before we could walk. Jay's not going to suddenly stop shoplifting, Carlos isn't going to suddenly have manners, and Evie's not going to stop cheating on her exams just because one overly optimistic prince hopes we'll be different. But there's something about Ben's big doe eyes, how he looks right at you all innocent, that makes him seem like an okay guy, even if he is Beast's son. He did make a funny joke about his dad shedding on the couch (at least it was kind of funny).

# HIS GIRLFRIEND, AUDREY?

There's nothing funny about her, except maybe her tight, tense smile. She's kind of the worst. Turns out she's Aurora's (Sleeping Beauty's) daughter, and she was sure I knew that within two seconds of stepping out of the car. We hadn't even grabbed our suitcases when she started insulting Evie, telling her that her mother's power didn't mean anything in Auradon, that she wasn't a princess, etc.

# I SUDDENLY GET WHY MY MOM COULDN'T STAND HER FAMILY. WHY SHE RISKED EVERYTHING TO CAST THAT SPELL ON AURORA SO MANY DECADES BEFORE.

If I had to listen to that kind of I'm-better-than-you-are-and-I-want-you-to-know-it snobbery for years, I'd have done the same thing. Maybe my mom wasn't spiteful . . . maybe she was just tired of listening to people like Aurora and her family talk.

AHHH!

I FORGOT THE MOST IMPORTANT PART.

Today we met the Fairy Godmother, owner of the magic wand that will help my mother bend both good and evil to her will. She didn't have the thing on her, and she wasn't really up for a line of questioning, but at least now we know we're close. If she's here, teaching at Auradon Prep, the wand can't be too far away. I just have to do a little more digging....

Uggghhh. I'm going to be sick.
I'm sitting in my new dorm
room, which looks like it
was decorated by
Cinderella's interior
designer. THINK PINK.
THINK THROW PILLOWS
AND EMBROIDERY AND
FLOWERS EVERYWHERE.

There are pink and white canopies above each of our beds (BTW, I'm rooming with Evie) and white dressers and dainty flowered curtains and all that gross stuff. It looks nothing like my room at home. As soon as we got here, I made Evie pull down the shades and close the windows, which only helped a little bit. At least in this dim light I can pretend that this isn't the prissiest room ever.

**BUT SERIOUSLY: HOW AM I GOING TO STAY HERE, EVEN FOR A FEW WEEKS? I'VE BEEN HERE TEN MINUTES AND I'M ALREADY DROWNING IN CHEERFULNESS.**

History of
Woodsmen
and Pirates

Enchanted
FORESTRY

Bad Fairies

Mathematics

Lunch/Recess

Grammar

History
of Auradon

Safety Rules for
the Internet

Remedial
Goodness
101

**Remedial Goodness 101?!?!** *Yeah. Right.* Is that really a class?

All of us—Jay, Carlos, Evie, and me—we're all required to take this one. I think they created it just for us. Fairy Godmother is the teacher, and I can only imagine what we're supposed to be learning. How to enchant birds and chipmunks. How to sing out windows about happy, wishful things. How to make seven dwarfs worship you. How to tame a beast.

Yeah. Right.
So that is happening.

IT'S TOTALLY WEIRD seeing Carlos, Jay, and Evie in Auradon. Carlos looks like a drowned rat next to all these preppy Auradon boys in their pleated pants and crisp shirts, and Jay has already stolen half the electronics in the school (seriously, we were just in his room, and he has a whole suitcase full of them). I think Evie secretly likes it here. I sometimes catch her smiling at some of the Auradon boys or flipping through the welcome packet Doug, Dopey's son, gave us. I wish she would just snap out of it. Now it feels weird to complain to her all the time. She just nods her head, like she gets what I'm saying, but I can tell she's thinking about something else. I mean, come on! What's so great about this place? Chad, Cinderella's son, that guy with the bad hair? Or all the classes and rules and people telling us to be *"good"* all the time, or wondering if we're *"GooD,"* or wanting to teach us how to be *"good"?* It's fine for now . . . but that's all it's fine for. We're leaving as soon as we get the wand.

I HATE THAT I'M QUOTING MY MOM HERE, BUT SHE WAS RIGHT ABOUT ONE THING:

DON'T. GET.* ATTACHED.

# TONIGHT WAS
# A BIG NIGHT.

The magic mirror got us what we needed—a location on the wand—so we should be able to break out of Auradon sooner rather than later (hopefully before Evie starts sewing the Auradon Prep crest on all of her clothes).

She used the mirror to zoom in on the wand, which is in a museum that Carlos says is just a few miles away. We can walk there, even if it means breaking curfew. Nothing we

HAVEN'T DONE BEFORE.
AND ALL THAT STEALING
JAY'S BEEN INTO? IT'LL
BE USEFUL TONIGHT,
WHEN WE'RE MOVING
THROUGH THE DARK,
JUST A FEW FEET FROM
THE WAND.

GOTTA GO—we're off to FIND
THE Museum of Cultural History.
WHATEVER THAT IS.

# I CAN'T BELIEVE WHAT HAPPENED AT THE MUSEUM. HOW QUICKLY THINGS WENT HORRIBLY, TERRIBLY WRONG.

We got to the museum right on schedule. There was only one guard in the front, manning it during the off hours. Perfect. Ideal. It was the first time I used my mom's spell book, and it was even better than I expected. I recited the sleeping spell to bring the guard over to my mother's spinning wheel, where he pricked his finger and fell unconscious. Then I recited another spell to open the door to the museum. After a brief and disturbing visit to the Gallery of Villains—more on that later—we were in the Wand Gallery where Fairy Godmother's wand was on display. We were right there—just ten feet away from it. It was covered in this perfect blue light.

If I told anyone this story, they'd be like:
• • • • • • • • • • • • • •

That's incredible.
What happened next?!?!

How did you get the magic wand
that you traveled miles and
risked everything for?

You couldn't have
possibly messed that up?!?

Those are questions for Jay. I was standing there, looking at the wand, thinking about all the different security systems that must've been in place around it. Were there laser beams that would shoot from the ceiling and cook us like burnt toast? Were there invisible force fields? Secret agents that would burst out from behind closed doors? That's what was going through *my* head as I was staring at that wand . . . but Jay? All he was thinking was: *I can't let Mal upstage me. After all her spells and fancy tricks getting into the museum, this is my turn to shine. I have one chance to show everyone*

# I'M THE BEST THIEF THE ISLE OF THE LOST HAS EVER KNOWN.

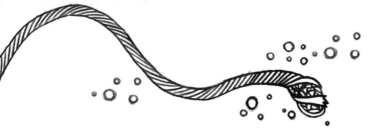

At least that's what I imagine he was thinking. What else would cause a person to lunge, without even hesitating, and try to grab one of the most valuable, powerful objects in all of Auradon?

# THEN: SCREECHING, SCREECHING, HORRIBLE WAILING. JAY TRIGGERED THE ALARM. HE COULDN'T BREAK THROUGH THE FORCE FIELD SURROUNDING IT, BUT HE DID WAKE UP THE GUARD FROM HIS DEEP, DREAMLESS SLEEP, AND WE ALL HAD TO RUN FOR OUR LIVES.

Literally. If it wasn't for Carlos thinking fast and answering the guard's phone to say everything was okay, we would've gotten caught. Now we're back in the dorms, without the wand, and without any other way of getting it. We can't break in again. We won't be able to get through that force field. It's too strong.

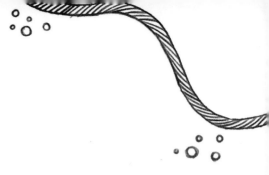

OUR ONLY HOPE? INSTEAD OF GOING TO THE WAND, WE BRING THE WAND TO US.....

# THE WEIRDEST THING HAPPENED WHEN I WAS IN THE MUSEUM.

Evie, Carlos, Jay, and I were wandering around the Gallery of Villains when I looked up and saw my mom. She was standing right there, towering above me, her scepter pointed at the sky. They had statues of everyone's parents, but this one was different. She looked so terrifying the rest of my friends just left and started searching for the wand in the other end of the east wing. They were so creeped out.

## The future rests on your shoulders.

That's what she said to me before I left the island. That she wanted me to be rotten like her, to call up the powers of evil the same way she did, to bring down the United States of Auradon. When I was standing there, looking at that statue of her, it was like I was back in her house, under her roof, listening to all her rules. I could hear her telling me what to do.

BE EVIL
LIKE ME, BE
RUTHLESS
AND
ROTTEN
AND MAD....

# Sometimes I wonder if that's who I am, though. I've thought about being

an artist, a singer, a designer . . . maybe even helping Evie with her fashion line. World domination was never at the top of my list. Maybe it doesn't matter, though. Being evil is the only way we know, and it's definitely the only way to make my mom proud. I'm her only daughter, and she wanted a mini Maleficent—that's why I'm named after her. She always told me I had to continue her legacy and work as hard as I could to dismantle the leadership in Auradon. How many times has she told me what Aurora's parents did to her, how they shamed her in front of the entire kingdom? How many more times can I hear about how the Beast robbed her of all the power she had and left her to rot on the Isle of the Lost? I know she's right, that they deserve to be punished, but still . . . wouldn't it be nice if, just for once, she gave me a choice? *If my future wasn't something she owned?*

LOOK AT YOU
LOOK at ME

I DON'T KNOW
WHO TO BE

MOTHER

IS IT WRONG
IS IT RIGHT

TO BE A THIEF IN
THE NIGHT?

MOTHER
TELL ME WHAT TO DO

Don't you want to be evil like me? Don't you want to be cruel? Don't you want to be nasty and brutal and cool?

Don't YOU WANT to be HEARTLESS and hardened as stone? Don't you want to be finger-lickin' EVIL TO THE BONE?

# REMEDIAL GOODNESS IS THE. WORST.CLASS. EVER.

# TOTAL SNOOZE INDUCER. My only chance at keeping

my eyes open is DRAWING IN MY JOURNAL, which, thankfully, Fairy
Godmother hasn't confiscated yet. As long as I throw my hand up
every once in a while and answer a question, she leaves me alone.
But still . . . We have to get the wand soon, because I don't think I
can stand much more of this.

YOU'RE WALKING THROUGH THE WOODS WHEN YOU SEE A PIG IN A STRAW HOUSE. DO YOU

A.) BANG ON THE DOOR AND DEMAND THE PIG LET YOU IN,

B.) THREATEN TO BLOW THE PIG'S HOUSE DOWN,

C.) TURN HIM INTO BACON, OR

Yum...

D.) KEEP WALKING?

# YOU DISCOVER TWO YOUNG CHILDREN ALL ALONE IN THE FOREST. DO YOU

A.) HELP THEM FIND THEIR WAY HOME,

B.) SELL THEM TO THE WITCH WHO LIVES BY THE RIVER,

C.) EMPTY THEIR POCKETS—THEY MIGHT HAVE SOMETHING VALUABLE ON THEM—OR

D.) JUMP OUT FROM BEHIND A TREE AND SCARE THEM?

# I FORGOT TO MENTION THE ONE GOOD PART OF REMEDIAL GOODNESS CLASS.

So Fairy Godmother is going on about our choices, and how important they are, when her daughter, Jane, walks in. The girl looked like she'd just entered a lion's den. She kept staring at us like we'd pounce on her at any moment and eat her alive. I guess Fairy Godmother has been telling her stories about our parents for years. How cunning and evil and scary they are (I can't say it's not true). But it was funny, as I was watching her hide behind her mom, those big blue eyes staring back at us, I got an idea. If she's the Fairy Godmother's daughter, she might be able to get her wand. . . .

See Jane. See Jane cower.
See Jane help Mal get
what she wants.

**YES!!!**

# Jay and Carlos have started playing tourney,

this game that all the Auradon students are into. And now Evie wants to join the cheer squad. Soooooo lame. I hate to admit it, though, but Jay's almost as good at tourney as he is at stealing. But Carlos . . . well, he's not exactly the most coordinated of villains. They weren't even five minutes into the game and he was on the ground, his hands over his head, getting trampled by the other players.

This school might actually kill him.

But never fear, Carlos! Enter a shining Auradon knight: Ben. The coach wanted to cut Carlos from the team, but Ben convinced him not to. He promised to train with Carlos until he got good enough to play with the others. I don't know if that's even possible, but Ben seemed eager to help . . . maybe a little too eager, you know? I keep wondering what's in it for him. Why is he being so nice to Carlos? To all of us? There has to be some other motive, something he wants from him—why else would he take the time to do that?

# Then, even weirder: after the tourney practice, Ben saw me

at my locker. I'd tagged the front of it with LONG LIVE EVIL, just like
we used to do on the island. I was turning to go, and he grabbed my
arm. I thought he was going to lecture me about vandalizing school
property, say some garbage about respecting Auradon Prep, blah
blah blah, but he didn't. He just looked at me with those big clear
eyes and asked *if I'd enrolled in art classes. Something
about me being talented and not wanting that to
go to waste. I was like . . . seriously?!? Is this guy
for real!??* Why does he care so much about what I'm doing at
Auradon Prep? Why would he even suggest that? I know what a
normal kid would say: he's just trying to be nice, he's trying to help.
But if my mom taught me anything, she taught me to always be
suspicious of people's motives. I'm just not sure I buy his whole
"nice guy" act.

So my plan has officially been set in motion. I followed Jane into the bathroom today and found her all mopey and teary-eyed over the sink. She kept staring at her reflection in the mirror, looking at her dull, lifeless hair like she was in a bad shampoo commercial. I've been watching her around school. She seems friendless, coasting from one class to another, alone. It seemed like a good opportunity . . . maybe the perfect opportunity.

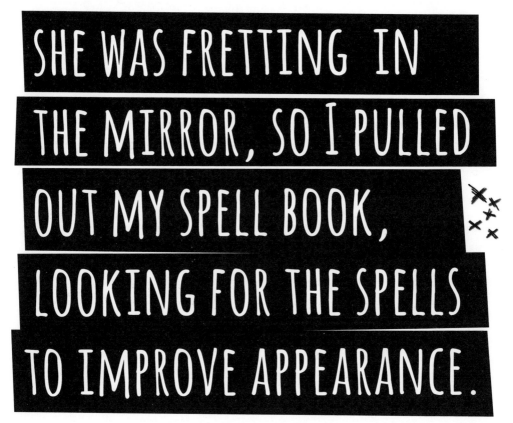

SHE WAS FRETTING IN THE MIRROR, SO I PULLED OUT MY SPELL BOOK, LOOKING FOR THE SPELLS TO IMPROVE APPEARANCE.

It's kind of funny, I never noticed how many there are. Spells to make your teeth straight, spells to get rid of pimples and freshen your breath. Anyway, I found the spells for hair and voila! Within seconds, Jane had a long, wavy do. She squealed, she was so excited.

•  •  •  •  •  •  •  •  •  •  •  •  •  •  •  •  •

Then, of course, she started peering over my shoulder at the spell book, wondering if I could make her nose different. Girl has major insecurity issues. I told her I couldn't (a small lie) but that she should ask her mother, Headmistress and Fairy Godmother Extraordinaire. Couldn't she use her magic wand on Jane? I mean, she Bibbidi-Bobbidi-Booed Cinderella. Gave her a completely new look. And speaking of using the wand, whenever that happens, could I please, pretty please, be there to watch?

BEAUTY FROM THE

COMES

INSIDE???

# Apparently Jane's mom has a new rule

about magic-wand makeovers. She's doesn't do them anymore. Instead she believes beauty comes from the inside, not the outside (way to flip-flop on that issue, FG). In fact, she doesn't even use the wand that much, which is probably why it's in the museum in the first place.

///////////////////////////////////////////////////////////////

So Jane promised she'd ask her to use the wand on her, that she'd beg her, really, and try to get her to change her mind.

///////////////////////////////////////////////////////////////

She told me I could come along and witness the big event when it happens, which, hopefully, will be soon.

Then, as soon as I'm there in the room with them, I'll make a grab for it. Jane's already on my side. Fairy Godmother won't expect it, not when she's so focused on the new and improved Jane.

## THIS SHOULD BE EASY . . . LIKE TAKING CANDY FROM A BABY. BUT WAY, WAY BETTER. I'LL SHOW MY MOM WHAT I'M CAPABLE OF.

# Evie's totally
## crushing on Chad.

Chad, as in Prince Charming Junior, as in Cinderella's Son.

It's been painful to watch. Sure, Chad is tall and blond and an athlete and popular, but he's also missing the keys to the castle. Read: he's dumb. Like, *really* dumb. **Now she's doing his chem homework for him.** She told me he wanted to meet her under the bleachers after class, and when she got there, he was being all sweet and charming (it *is* in his genes . . . ick), telling her how smart she is. He kept leaning in like he was going to kiss her. He never did. What *did* he do? He shoved his backpack at her and asked her to do all his homework. Only then, when she's finished, will he hang out with her. He even called her "babe."

# DID I MENTION I CAN'T STAND THIS GUY?!?

I don't know, sometimes I worry all that talk from Evie's mom about princes and kings has messed with her head. The Evil Queen is obsessed with Evie marrying some rich prince. She wants to live in a castle in Auradon with a giant suite for the mother-in-law. (If I'm living with my mom when I'm older, please kill me.) The thing is, Evie is smart—she's one of the smartest, most talented people I know. But she's been using her mom's magic mirror to cheat on tests. She even told me she was pretending to Chad that she wasn't as smart as she is, hoping that might get him to like her. It's making me mad just writing about it. Evie's so much better than him. She's smart and funny and beautiful and talented and amazing.

# IF ONLY SHE REALIZED THAT.

"IF A BOY CAN'T SEE THE BEAUTY THAT'S WITHIN, THEN HE ISN'T WORTH IT."

—Fairy Godmother

# YES, THAT'S A DIRECT QUOTE.

And technically I agree with it, like really agree with it (I wish Evie got all her advice from FG). I only wish she didn't say it to Jane. Because that means my plan is off, done, finished, not going to work. Jane asked her mom about the makeover, saying that she wanted it to help her get a boyfriend, and Fairy Godmother told her no way. Jane's been hanging in our room ever since (moping is the right word, I guess), being sad about the no-makeover policy, even if she's still obsessed with her hair.

The thing I don't get? What's so great about having a boyfriend? Why is it this big goal everyone's after? The way Evie and Jane are acting, you'd think getting a boyfriend magically solves all your problems, makes you do better in school and have more friends, and just makes everything awesome. Look, I've never had one, but as far as I can tell, boyfriends just create more problems. Evie's lying around, doing Chad's homework, and Jane feels lame and sad just thinking about boys. I'd honestly rather sit in my room, drawing in this book, than be out there dealing with that nonsense.

But back to the wand.
I have to figure out something else now that Jane isn't of use. If we go back to the museum, we risk getting caught. There has to be some other way to get it. . . .

# BOYFRIENDS

- - - - - - - - - - - - - - - - - - - - - - - - - - - - - - - -

## CONS

- I'd have to deal with him
- If I don't like his friends, I'd have to deal with them, too
- I might have to do his homework for him
- Less time to hang out with my friends
- Less time to draw in my sketchbook
- Less time for plotting evil
- Less freedom

# PROS

- I can say I have a boyfriend

- Other people might think it's cool I have a BOYFRIEND (who cares, though?)

- If he's really GREAT (likelihood: 0%) it might be fun

**WORD HAS SPREAD ABOUT JANE'S HAIR.** Just a few hours ago this girl Lonnie, Mulan's daughter, came to our room, wanting Evie and me to give her a new look. I wasn't interested, but then she sweetened the deal (girl after my own heart). Fifty dollars for a new haircut. Evie wanted to give her a fancy hairstyle, but Lonnie wanted something "cool" like mine.

I know I'm supposed to hate everyone in Auradon, all these elite princesses and princes, these goody two-shoes who cast out my mom and all her friends. And I do. But when Jane and Lonnie were in our room, just hanging out, it wasn't completely awful having them there. Lonnie's even . . . well, kind of cool. Or really . . . she thinks *I'm* cool, which makes me like her for having good taste. And Jane, as painfully insecure as she is, makes me laugh. Lonnie tore her skirt trying to make her outfit look a little more like mine, and then Jane tore her skirt, too. Half a second later she looked panicked, like she couldn't believe she'd just ripped up her clothing. She said something about her mom being mad at her. It's like she wants to be bad like us . . . but no matter how hard she tries, she just can't.

about jane's hair

I DON'T KNOW. I GUESS IT JUST WASN'T TERRIBLE, HANGING OUT WITH THEM. MAYBE IT WAS EVEN KIND OF . . . NICE.

DID I JUST USE THE WORD NICE?!?! GROSS. I THINK THIS PLACE IS GETTING TO ME.

I'VE BEEN SITTING HERE FOR THE LAST TWO HOURS, THUMBING THROUGH MY MOM'S SPELL BOOK, TRYING TO FIGURE OUT IF

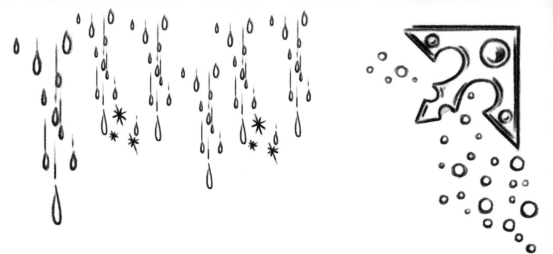

there's another way to get to the wand. Sure, there are spells on changing hairstyles and poisoning apples, but there's not one single spell for thievery (I'm talking ninja-style, heist-level thievery, not the petty kind Jay gets away with). No way to break a force field, either. My Mom said all the answers were in here . . . but then where are they? How am I supposed to get into the museum again, get past the guard, break a force field and turn off an alarm, then leave without anyone realizing the wand is missing? How is that even possible?

To make everything worse, it's like Evie doesn't even care. She's spent the entire night working on Chad's homework, using her magic mirror to get all the right answers to the chem questions. When I asked her why she was even bothering, she barely glanced up from her books. Then she mumbled something about Chad being cute.

# I MEAN ...

## I'D ASK JAY OR CARLOS FOR HELP, but it's taken

Jay less than a minute to become captain of the Auradon Prep tourney team (or practically—the coach loves him). I saw him walking around in his jersey before, talking to his teammates about a big game that's coming up. And Carlos? He's been hiding out in his room playing video games and tackling his dog fears. Apparently he met Dude, this cute little pup, who's helping him learn to love again (baby steps, baby steps).

So it looks like it's all on me. If I don't figure this out, no one else is going to. And maybe Evie doesn't care if the Evil Queen is furious with her, and maybe Carlos isn't terrified of Cruella, but failure is not an option for me. Not with my mom. They don't call her the Mistress of All Evil for nothing.

OHHHHKAAAAAAy.
So maybe I was
a little hard on
my friends.
What can I say?
I'm my mother's
daughter.
TOUGH LOVE is
all I know.

When I was freaking out about the wand and how we were going
to get it, Carlos, Evie, and Jay all confessed that they were worried
about going back to the island, too. Even if my mom is the worst villain
there, Jafar wouldn't be thrilled if Jay didn't do what he said. And there's
no way Carlos wants to return to his mom and deal with all her crazy
talking to dead dog pelts and whatnot. Even Evie was stressed. She
just never told me until tonight.

The thing is . . . we are all in this together, even if it doesn't feel that
way sometimes. We came here together, and we have to leave here
together, with or without the wand. It might sound cheesy (fine, it *is*
a little cheesy), but when all four of us were in our room tonight, we
stood there and made a pact. Nothing will come between us. We're
going to get the wand and bring it back to the Isle of the Lost. We can
do this, we *will* do this, especially if we stick together.

Oh! And! SUPER IMPORTANT: Evie somehow forgot to mention she got insider info from Doug. Apparently the wand is used during the coronation ceremony. When Ben is crowned KING, Fairy Godmother blesses him with it or something.

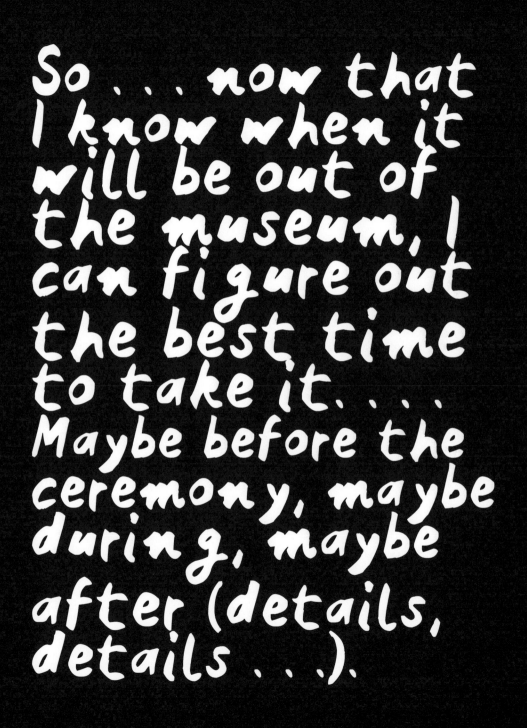

So . . . now that I know when it will be out of the museum, I can figure out the best time to take it. . . . Maybe before the ceremony, maybe during, maybe after (details, details . . .).

Ben dropped by just a little while ago, after the whole "let's stick together" talk with Jay, Carlos, and Evie. He wanted to know if I had any questions about Auradon Prep. *As a matter of fact I do . . .* I thought. I asked him all about the coronation ceremony. It turns out Evie was right—everyone in school is invited. I specifically asked if the four of us could stand in the front row, right beside him. Wouldn't that be great? Wouldn't that show the new and improved union between Auradon and the Isle of the Lost? How good and innocent all us children are?

He said it just. Wasn't. Possible. Apparently the front row is reserved for VIPs. Only very important people, like Belle, the Beast, Fairy Godmother, Ben, and . . . wait for it . . . Ben's girlfriend. So even if Ben said nope, I can't stand in the front row—he really meant yes. Because the VIP thing isn't an obstacle. Maybe right *now* Audrey is Ben's girlfriend, but maybe by the time the coronation rolls around it will be someone else. Someone smarter. Someone tougher. Someone with a little more edge. Someone who knows a love spell.

# MAYBE BY THE TIME THE CORONATION ROLLS AROUND . . . IT'LL BE ME.

PRINCE BEN.
KING BEN.
BENNYBOO.
LITTLE BENNY FOO FOO.
OL' BENNY BOY.
THE BMOC (BIG MAN ON CAMPUS).
MY FUTURE BOYFRIEND.

# Chocolate CHIP cookies.

Who knew about these things? They're, like, special snacks that parents make for their kids? Sometimes they do it to cheer them up when they're sad? (Side note: parents care when their kids are sad????)

I'D SERIOUSLY NEVER HEARD ABOUT THEM BEFORE. NEITHER HAD JAY, CARLOS, OR EVIE.

# BUT LET ME START FROM THE BEGINNING. After Ben told us about the

coronation, we went down to the school kitchen to make your run-of-the-mill magic cookies. I'd found this love spell in my mom's spell book (she was right . . . it does have all the answers). The recipe was for cookies that would make someone fall hopelessly in love with the first person they saw after eating them. The plan: bake a few of these cookies, give one to Ben, and then just stand there and wait for the effects to take hold. As long as I'm the first person he sees, Audrey won't have a chance anymore. Ben will fall truly, madly, deeply in love with me. He will want me as his girlfriend . . . and his date to the coronation. It's my ticket to the wand. Evil genius, right??

So we followed the recipe, and the cookies are baking now. They should be ready any minute. But the thing is . . . while we were down there in the kitchen, Lonnie came in, looking for a midnight snack. She started talking about how we should add chocolate chips, and didn't we know what chocolate chip cookies were? Her mother used to bake them for her when she was feeling sad. Apparently her mom would sit there with Lonnie and talk to her and make jokes, trying to cheer her up. The cookies would come out of the oven warm, with melted, ooey-gooey chocolate chips, and her mom would serve them to her with a glass of milk.

## It's just . . . I hate to admit it, but that was kind of hard

to hear. Things are different on the Isle of the Lost. Maybe even more different than I initially thought. On the Isle of the Lost, cookies and cakes are mostly used for evil. Potions can be mixed into the batter, poisons can be hidden in the frosting of a cupcake or cinnamon bun. None of our parents bake us cookies as a treat. In fact . . . no one's parents would ever give them a "special snack." Nobody sits down with me after school and helps me with my homework. No one asks me how my day was. No one cares.

It's the same for Jay, Evie, and Carlos. As Lonnie kept going on and on about her mom, and how sweet she was to her, I could feel my friends getting uncomfortable. They must've been thinking the same thing I was. That they'd been missing out on something they didn't even know existed. I don't ever remember my mom hugging me. I don't remember her checking in to see how I was feeling, or trying to cheer me up when I was sad about school or my friends or anything. In fact, my mom is usually the reason I feel sad.

## She's always criticizing me, always telling me I could cast more spells, that I could be more evil. That I should be like her.

## Better.

Whatever . . . it's not worth thinking about anymore. I can't change what happened in the past.

I still can't get Lonnie's words out of my head. She looked at us, tears in her eyes, and said: *I just, I thought . . . even villains love their kids.*

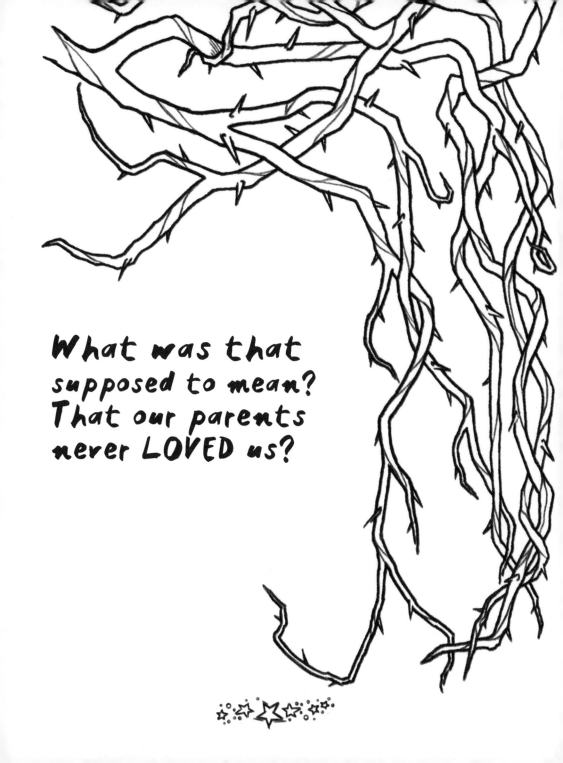

What was that
supposed to mean?
That our parents
never LOVED us?

# IT HAPPENED.
# IT'S DONE,
# FINITO, MISSION
# ACCOMPLISHED.
# BEN IS OFFICIALLY
# IN LOVE WITH ME.

I should be happy. Overjoyed and blushing and elated.
But as suspected, this whole boyfriend thing is
waaaaaaaay overrated. It started like this: I found
Ben in the hall after class and offered him one of the
magic, love-inducing cookies. At first he didn't want it,

said something about not liking to eat much before a big tourney game. Then I batted my eyelashes and gave him a sad puppy dog face. *I completely understand*, I said. *Be careful of treats offered by kids of villains. I'm sure every kid in Auradon learns that one, right?* He fell for the guilt trip. Sucker! I had barely finished the sentence before he grabbed the cookie from my hand and took a bite. Then I just stood there and let the spell do all the work.

Within minutes, he's noticing the gold flecks in my irises. He's smiling all goofy, staring, his eyes bulging out of his head. Then he told me he felt like singing my name, and almost started to shout "Mal!" but I covered up his mouth. It was humiliating.

I had to go to the tourney game right after that. Technically it was Evie's idea—she wanted to see Chad, Prince Harming My Friend's Self-Esteem, in all his glory. *Please don't make me go alone*, she begged. *I can't sit there by myself. I'll look like a total dork.*

# WHAT CAN I SAY? FRIENDS DON'T LET FRIENDS LOOK LIKE TOTAL DORKS.

The good news: Carlos is getting better. He's decent even—apparently all that training with Ben actually helped. He ran a pass straight across the field, dodging all of the Sherwood players, then chucked it at Chad, who helped score a win. And Jay's definitely soaking up all the attention. I've spent years watching people yell *at* him ("Stop!" "Thief!" "He has my purse!"), but I've never seen so many people yelling *for* him. Every time he got the ball the crowd stood up, cheering, screaming his name. And Bennyboo? Little Benny Foo Foo? He wasn't so bad, either. In fact, he's pretty great at tourney. The team beat the Sherwood Falcons 3–2.

# WHAT'S NOT GREAT, THOUGH, IS BEN'S COMPLETE LACK OF SUBTLETY.

Yes, he's my boyfriend now (he made that clear in front of everybody), and, yes, I put a spell on him that has turned him all **googly-eyed and crazy about me,** telling me how pretty and smart and fun I am (I'll admit to it—that is all my fault). But this **love is over-the-top ridiculous.** I don't know if I messed up the recipe or what, but today, after every time he scored, he put his hand on his heart and looked up into the stands at me. He must've blown me a hundred kisses. Then, as soon as the game ended, he burst into another song and dance, and got the entire crowd to help him spell out my name.

# GIVE ME A B . . . GIVE ME AN A . . . GIVE ME AN R . . . GIVE ME AN F.

I LOVE YOU MAL

There was one good thing about all of this: Audrey is on the cheer squad, so she witnessed the whole scene. Her face was getting redder and redder as the game went on. Every smile from Ben, every time he blew me a kiss—she looked more and more like a cherry tomato about to explode. By the time he was finished serenading me she'd grabbed Chad, giving him a big, obvious peck on the lips. *Chad is my boyfriend now!* she yelled at Ben. *And I'm going to coronation with him! So I don't need your pity date!* So, I did it. I got Ben to fall in love with me, and most importantly I'm now Ben's date to the coronation. Which means I have a first-row, wand-adjacent seat.

# WHY, THANK YOU, AUDREY. YOU JUST MADE MY LIFE A WHOLE LOT EASIER.

# OH . . . I DIDN'T MENTION THE ONE KIND OF AWFUL THING ABOUT

Audrey's new guy. Evie is crushed. It was hard for her to even look
at them together. As the entire school was cheering and running
onto the field, celebrating Auradon Prep's win, I had to pull Evie
aside so no one would see she was on the verge of tears.

I hate everything about this. I hate that Evie's upset, and I hate that
she can't see that she's a billion times better than that dim-witted
fool. I hate that she's still doing his homework for him and that he
doesn't even appreciate it. I just . . . I hate seeing my friend so upset.
Did I mention that already?

Evie's beautiful and can sew and do three back handsprings, one
after the other. She's an amazing designer and she's a good friend . . .
the best I've ever had. I can't wait until the coronation. I'll be there
as Ben's date. I'll get the wand and then we'll be free of Auradon
Prep, with all its rules and all its prissy princes and princesses. And
Evie will finally be free of Chad.

FINALLY FREE

# THIS WHOLE BOYFRIEND THING IS GETTING OUT OF CONTROL. JUST BEFORE, WHEN I WAS WALKING TO ENCHANTED FORESTRY,

Ben cornered me. Turns out he wants to go on a date. Like an official date-y date, where he picks me up and takes me somewhere special, and we sit, gazing into each other's eyes, probably over a plate of fancy food in a stuffy restaurant.

This was just supposed to be about the coronation. I'd be his date, and I'd keep up the whole lovey-dovey act until then. But now I have to spend time with him, time that could be spent drawing or hanging out with Evie or plotting. Ugh. It's not that he's a bad guy . . . it's just the opposite. He's so squeaky clean. Everything about him is so happy and pure and optimistic. I see the glass half empty; he sees it half full. I see a dull gray sky with clouds, and he's going on telling everyone how excited he is about the rain. I see my friends as villains, kids bent on revenge . . . and Ben? He sees us all as innocents. He still believes we're capable of good.

# WOW. I COULDN'T HELP LAUGHING, WRITING THAT.

I just . . . I don't want to spend any more time with him than I already have to, you know? Yes, he's a good guy, and it was cool of him to help Carlos conquer his dog fear and get better at tourney. But if I hang out with him too much, all that Auradon cheer might rub off on me. I'll lose my edge. I have to be on guard. I have to remember the ultimate plan.

# I GOTTA STOP HERE, THOUGH. I'M OFF TO FIND EVIE. IF ANYONE KNOWS HOW TO PREPARE FOR A DATE WITH A PRINCE, IT'S HER. . . .

# I'VE BEEN LOOKING THROUGH MY SPELL BOOK ALL AFTERNOON, CONSIDERING

the shrinking spell (which can turn a giant into a dwarf) or the mute spell (to take away someone's voice). If I didn't think it'd be obvious if I cursed Chad, I would start reciting one of them right now. How awesome would it be to see him turned into a newt? Or have him slip away into a deep sleep? Or if he was shrunken down to the height of Sleepy or Grumpy or Doc?

~~~~~~~~~~~~~~~~~~~~~~~~~~~~~~~~~~~~~~~~~~~~~~

Because things have gotten so much worse. After all the homework Evie did for him, he ratted her out to their chem teacher, Mr. Delay. At some point (after she gave him his work back, of course) he told Mr. Delay that Evie had been using her magic mirror to get the right answers. So when they were in class today, taking a test, and Evie reached for her purse, Mr. Delay confronted her about it. He was convinced she was going to cheat on the test (I plead the Fifth on that one). Then he told her he was going to have her expelled.

~~~~~~~~~~~~~~~~~~~~~~~~~~~~~~~~~~~~~~~~~~~~~~

Chad just sat there, smirking. Mr. Delay said something about the honor code, and how important it was that some students still respected it. If it wasn't for Doug, Evie might be heading back to the Isle of the Lost right now. He was the only one who stood up for her. He convinced Mr. Delay to let her take the test again to see if she could pass on her own . . . which she did.

## BECAUSE SHE'S EVIE. BECAUSE SHE'S SO SMART AND CAPABLE. AT LEAST SOME PEOPLE HERE RECOGNIZE THAT.

# DOS AND DON'TS
## FOR DATING A PRINCE
### (aka: Advice from Evie)

-=-=-=-=-=-=-=-=-=-=-=-=-=-=-=-=-=-=-

IN CASE I EVER HAVE ANOTHER DATE WITH A PRINCE-HA HA HA!!!

- **DO USE MAKEUP** to accentuate your features.

- **DO HAVE A STYLE** that's all your own (we've seen the sparkly ball gown look 100x before).

- **DO LET THE PRINCE PLAN THE DATE.** You'll get to see how romantic he is.

- - - - - - - - - - - - - - - - - - -

- **DON'T BE NERVOUS.** Be confident, calm, and in control.

- **DON'T DO** his chem **HOMEWORK** for him. Ever.

# EVIE SPENT THE LAST HOUR TRANSFORMING ME BETTER THAN ANY SPELL COULD.

She's always been good at makeup, but she really outdid herself this time. She used this **sparkly purple liner** to make my eyes pop (Evie-speak for "stand out"). Then she brushed blush over my cheekbones and gave me some **plum lip gloss**. She must've spent a half hour going over my outfit, adding the perfect button here or the best pin there, then ripping different hems to make it look more edgy. She even let me borrow her favorite scarf.

I'm not used to wearing this much makeup, but I have to admit—it's really cool. I look like the best version of myself. Evie and I have always been different in that way. She's used to consulting her mom's magic mirror, and the Evil Queen has probably told her a thousand times that she has to dress to impress, that she must be the fairest of them all. But I usually just put on some lip balm and head out the door. It's kind of cool to dress up, though, even if I'm just going out with a fake boyfriend who's under a really intense love spell. Ben probably wouldn't notice if I was wearing a trash bag.

PS: Is it weird that
I'm kind of nervous?

. . . . . . . . . . . . . . . . . . . . . . . . . . . . .

While I was getting ready, though, we ended up talking about my mom. It's hard not to think of her now, when I'm just days away from getting the wand. I want her to be proud of me, but the longer I'm here at Auradon Prep, the more I realize that everything is always on her terms. She loves me, I believe she does, at least in her own way. But is "her own way" good enough? What happens when all of Auradon is in her control, when her power is unchallenged? How will she treat me then?

# I CAN'T THINK ABOUT THIS. NOT RIGHT NOW. BEN IS SUPPOSED TO COME GET ME IN A LITTLE BIT....

I don't know where to start. I remember every minute of our date last night, every word spoken between us. I keep running through it again and again in my head . . . it's like I'm afraid I'll forget.

• • • • • • • • • • • • • • • • • • • • • • • • • • •

He picked me up at my dorm room, and I immediately noticed **he seemed different**. He didn't dress as preppy as he normally does. His hair was a little messy, like he'd just rolled out of bed. And as soon as he saw me he smiled. *For the first time I know the difference between pretty and beautiful*, he said. We went downstairs to the quad where he'd parked his Vespa.

# HE GAVE ME AN EXTRA HELMET, A PURPLE ONE WITH A ROSE PAINTED ON IT, AND WE TOOK THE BACK ROADS TO AN ENCHANTED LAKE ON THE OTHER SIDE OF AURADON. I REMEMBER HOW MY CHEEK PRESSED

AGAINST HIS BACK AS THE VESPA SPED AROUND CURVES. HOW TIGHTLY I HAD TO HOLD ON TO HIM. THE ENDS OF MY HAIR WERE OUT OF THE HELMET AND THEY KEPT WHIPPING AROUND, FLYING EVERYWHERE AS THE WIND RUSHED PAST.

When we got to the enchanted lake we just hung out for a while. There's this cool bridge that looks out over the water, and the trees rise up around it. It might seem silly to say, but I've never seen so many colors in one place. Deep turquoise water, fuchsia flowers, and green everywhere. On the Isle of the Lost everything looks broken down. Even the trees have withered to a dark, lifeless brown. So Ben and I just stood there, talking, and at one point he told me a little about his speech for the coronation. He's planning to stand in front of everyone and tell them that it's time the people of Auradon embrace the children of the island. To give us the same chances that the children of Auradon had. *We do not become great by our strength, but by our compassion,* he'd said.

I didn't want to feel anything, I really didn't. But looking into Ben's eyes as he said those words—I could tell he actually believes them. That I deserve the same chances he had. That all my friends do.

I mean, it would be kind of great to go to a school where kids actually show up to class, where a lesson isn't interrupted by a fight every five minutes. A class where not everyone cheats on every exam. Like here, in Auradon, kids actually want to be something (besides evil). They talk about their futures and what it might be like to go to college, or have one of those massive palaces in the Auradon Hills. And they work hard. I mean, all the time—on the tourney field, in every class—even the cheer squad practices after school every day. And everyone's just so . . . *happy.* It's kind of cool sometimes.

I've been thinking about it . . . what Ben meant by that—us having the same chances he and all his friends had. What it would mean if we could stay here for a while. I would be able to take art classes, like he suggested, and Carlos and Jay would only get better at tourney. Evie might be able to start the clothing line she's always dreamed about. Everyone is already obsessed with all her designs.

. . . . . . . . . . . . . . . . . . . . . . . .

Anyway . . . Ben and I were sitting on a blanket by the lake, having a picnic, when we started talking about our parents. Ben keeps insisting we have a lot in common. It must be the love spell, because I still can't see it. He's going to be king. His parents are the poster parents for goodness. Belle probably sang him lullabies every night, and the Beast probably helped him with his homework and tossed around the tourney ball with him whenever he was bored. My mom? I don't think she even knows that I draw. She's never asked to look at my sketches, and she definitely hasn't ever sung me a lullaby (unless you count evil chants—she would use them on me whenever I stayed up too late). But Ben told me it doesn't matter, that we're not automatically like our parents. We get to choose who we're going to be. He looked into my eyes and said he could tell I wasn't evil.

. . . . . . . . . . . . . . . . . . . . . . . .

I MUST BE A TERRIFIC ACTRESS. I AM MY MOTHER'S DAUGHTER. SIXTEEN YEARS ON THAT ISLAND CAN'T BE ERASED JUST BECAUSE BEN WANTS THINGS TO BE DIFFERENT, TO BE BETTER. MAYBE I WANT THAT, TOO . . . WHO KNOWS. IT DOESN'T MATTER, THOUGH.

## WHAT I WANT DOESN'T MATTER. MY MOM NEEDS THE WAND. THERE'S NO WAY I CAN RETURN TO THE ISLE OF THE LOST UNLESS I HAVE IT.

• • • • • • • • • • • • • • • • • • • • • • • • • • • •

Anyway . . . we sat there for a while, and then Ben went swimming. He must've been underwater for at least five minutes because I was totally certain he had drowned. I jumped in to save him. One problem: I can't swim. So *he* actually ended up saving *me*.

////////////////////////////////////////////////////////////////////////////////////

It turns out he was getting a crystal from the bottom of the lake. He gave it to me. *I told you I love you,* he said. *What about you? Do you love me?*

## I TOLD HIM I DIDN'T KNOW WHAT LOVE FEELS LIKE.

*Maybe I can teach you* . . . he said.

////////////////////////////////////////////////////////////////////////////////////

I keep hearing his voice, hearing those words, whispered as he leaned in close to me. I still get this weird fluttering feeling in my stomach whenever I think of that moment between us . . . even just the idea of love.

## IT'S CRAZY, BUT A PART OF ME WANTS TO BELIEVE HE'S RIGHT. MAYBE HE CAN TEACH ME.

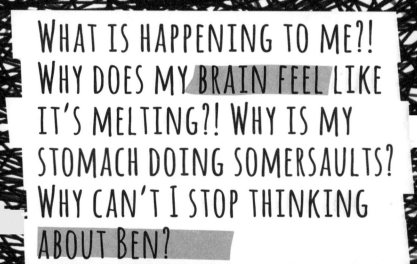

WHAT IS HAPPENING TO ME?!
WHY DOES MY BRAIN FEEL LIKE
IT'S MELTING?! WHY IS MY
STOMACH DOING SOMERSAULTS?
WHY CAN'T I STOP THINKING
ABOUT BEN?

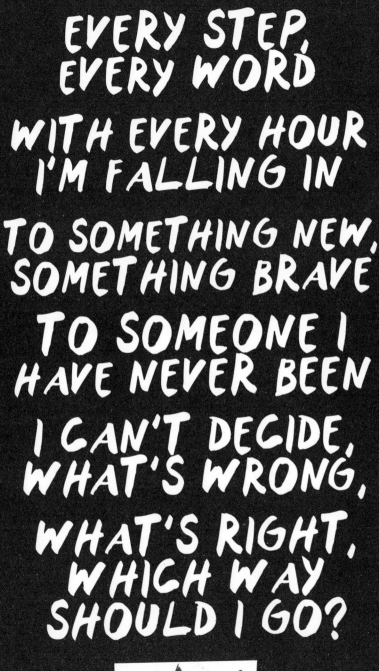

# ALSO, I HAD STRAWBERRIES FOR THE FIRST TIME.

They're delicious. So sweet and fresh . . . There's nothing like them on the Isle of the Lost. It's pretty sad—we missed out on a lot of pretty great things on the isle. Home not-so-sweet home.

Who cares, though, really. Ben only treated me so nicely because he's under a love spell, convinced that we're more alike than we are. I have to keep reminding myself that it wasn't real. Whatever happened on the date, whatever I felt, it was part of the love spell. Ben is going to be the king of Auradon. His parents are my mother's sworn enemies. There's no way he'd fall for me, of all girls, when he could be with someone like Audrey. They're both good. I'm evil. End of story.

////////////////////////////////////////////////////////////////////////////////

But . . . errrr . . . this is the tricky thing about magic. It felt so real. All of it. I remember being underneath the water, sure that I was going to drown, my legs kicking out, trying to keep me afloat. Then Ben was there, holding me in his arms, pulling me up to the shore. He'd draped his jacket over my shoulders and sat with me until I caught my breath. He was so close I thought he might even kiss me. Then he'd said it—that thing about teaching me what love feels like. . . .

I HAVE TO JUST LET IT GO.
I CAN'T THINK ABOUT THIS,
I WON'T. IT WASN'T REAL.
WHATEVER HE SAID, IT
WAS JUST THE LOVE SPELL
TALKING. I'M NOT GOING
TO THINK ABOUT IT AGAIN.
IT WASN'T REAL.

AM I CRAZY?

MAYBE WE
COULD HAPPEN

WILL YOU STILL
BE WITH ME WHEN
THE MAGIC
HAS RUN OUT?

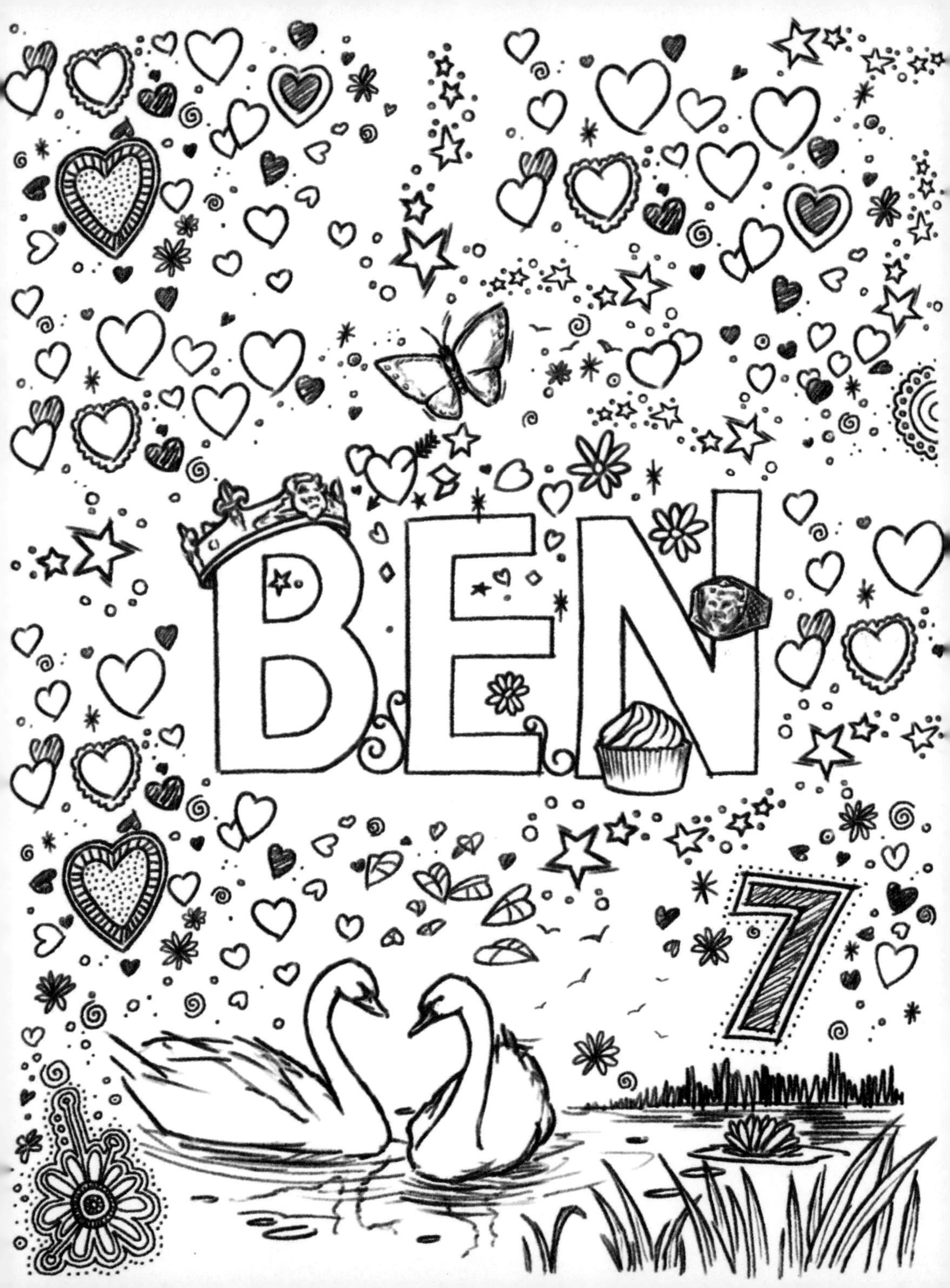
BEN
7

## I KNOW, I KNOW, I PROMISED MYSELF I WASN'T GOING TO WRITE ANY MORE ENTRIES ABOUT BEN.

•  •  •  •  •  •  •  •  •  •  •  •  •  •  •  •

And this isn't an entry about Ben. This is me . . . writing about how I want to write about Ben but I'm not going to. This is not about the date, or what he said to me, or how he held my hand in his. It's not about the way he looked at me with his big kind eyes and it's not–

•  •  •  •  •  •  •  •  •  •  •  •  •  •  •  •  •  •  •  •  •  •

You know what? I'm seriously not going to do this. I'm not going to think about that silly date anymore. I shouldn't. I'm stopping writing . . .

## RIGHT . . .

## NOW.

Sunday is Family Day at Auradon Prep—the day when all the students' parents and siblings show up for a party on the great lawn. They get to see the school, meet their kid's teachers, and schmooze with Belle and the Beast (every good citizen wants a picture with them for their mantle). There are four parents who can't attend, though, for, um . . . *obvious* reasons. Like they might just set the school on fire, or curse the queen, or send the entire kingdom into a sudden, endless night. So today Fairy Godmother arranged for Jay, Carlos, Evie, and me to have a very "special treat."

# I HONESTLY THINK A POP QUIZ IN REMEDIAL GOODNESS WOULD'VE BEEN MORE FUN.

Fairy Godmother pulled up the computer monitor and dialed our parents in. Live from the Isle of the Lost, it's . . . Family Day with Maleficent, Mistress of Evil! It was completely, terribly awful. She barely let the other parents talk, and she kept glaring into the lens, her eyes on me every second, asking me questions in code. *How long must Mommy wait to see you? You know Mommy's not good at waiting.* I spoke back to her in code, telling her about the coronation, and how she'd see me (read: the wand) sometime after that. But even that wasn't good enough. Then she wanted to know why it was taking so long, and couldn't she see me—er, the wand—sooner?

*For once it would be nice if she asked me something about myself. How about: Mal, I know you've been at a new school this month, how's that going? Or: Mal, how are your teachers? Have you made any friends? Or what about: Mal, are you homesick at all? I've missed you so much.*

Nope. Nothing. It's always about what I can do for her or how she can use me. Jay, Evie, and Carlos all fought with their parents, too. Cruella was disgusted when she heard about Carlos's new friend, Dude the dog, and the Evil Queen was too busy staring at herself in the mirror to even notice Evie. I hate it, but at times like these I can't stop picturing Lonnie's face when she realized our parents didn't bake us things, or sing us lullabies, or give us hugs when we were feeling sad.

I JUST . . . she'd started, tears in her eyes. I THOUGHT EVEN VILLAINS LOVED THEIR KIDS.

I'VE SEEN BEN A BUNCH OF TIMES SINCE OUR DATE. HE ALWAYS STOPS
at my locker to talk to me before class. Sometimes he just wants
to know how my day is going, other times he tells me a funny story
about Carlos and Dude. (Those two are inseparable these days.
Total BFFs.) He's been busy with tourney practice, and he's still
thinking I should add an art class to my schedule next semester. It's
always hard to look at him when he talks about next semester . . .
or about anything after the coronation. I feel like such a liar. I mean,
I'm good at lying. It's my strength (my forte, as my mom would say),
but wouldn't it be better to be known as an awesome artist, or for
my wardrobe, or pretty much anything else? Do I really want "lying"
to be the best thing about me? I just . . . I don't know anymore. . . .

After the coronation, when I finally get the wand, everything will be
different. At least I won't have to keep up this whole charade with
Ben anymore.

I've been thinking about what he said that night by the lake. Is it
true that we don't automatically become our parents? Do we really
get to choose who we want to be? And if that were true, if I did have
a choice, what would I decide?

I FEEL SICK. MY HANDS ARE SHAKING AND MY THROAT IS ALL SCRATCHY AND DRY. I MUST BE COMING DOWN WITH SOMETHING. I DON'T KNOW WHAT'S WRONG WITH ME, I SHOULD BE HAPPY. OVERJOYED.

## WE FINALIZED THE PLAN TONIGHT.

# WE MAPPED OUT THE AREA AROUND THE

cathedral where the coronation is being held, and we decided on each of our roles. I'll be the one to take the wand from Fairy Godmother's hands (obviously). Carlos will search the cars outside, looking for the same limo that drove us over the bridge into Auradon. When he finds it he'll alert Evie. I've given her a special atomizer my mom gave me. It looks like a perfume bottle, and with two good spritzes in the face, the driver will be unconscious. Jay will help escort me out of the cathedral, where the limo will be waiting for us. Then Carlos will take us home.

SIMPLE, RIGHT? THIS SHOULD BE EASY. It's what we've wanted since we got here, and we had to plan it now, while we were all together. Evie and Jay were pretty worried after talking to our parents. One thing was clear: if we don't come back to the Isle of the Lost with the wand, we shouldn't come back at all. There's no way our parents will be okay with us failing. Not at something so important.

So we're going to do this. On Friday, right at ten o'clock in the morning. We're going to steal the wand. And as soon as we bring it back to my mother, she'll break the spell cast on the Isle of the Lost. **All the villains will be set free. They'll rush into Auradon, looting and dragging the citizens from their houses**. They'll put the leaders of Auradon in prison, including Ben's parents, Belle and the Beast. **Then they'll ruin everything about this place that's beautiful and good.**

All that will happen just as soon as we carry out the plan. This is what we've wanted to do since we stepped onto the grounds of Auradon Prep. **This is what we're *supposed* to do**. It's just . . . I don't know. Things seem less certain now. If this is what is right, why does everything feel so wrong?

**how to break a love spell**

How to Break a Love Spell. Straight out of my mother's spell book, right after How to Open a Locked Door. The spell had another recipe, this one for a chocolate cupcake, to be eaten by the one under the influence of love. Two bites and they're free from all those intense feelings. **No more professing their undying affections to their beloved. No more gazing into their girlfriend's eyes or confessing their secrets. No more dates in enchanted forests or moonlight rides through Auradon. . . .**

out of my mother's spell book

Evie seemed surprised that I wanted to do this—set Ben free from the love spell. But it just seems so . . . wrong not to. When the villains storm Auradon, they'll look for Ben and his family first. They'll imprison them in the castle tower during the takeover. How will he fight back if he's stumbling around, confused about why the love of his life just betrayed his entire country? What if they hurt him?

## UGH . . . MY MOTHER WOULD KILL ME IF SHE EVER READ THIS.

I know, I know. I was raised a villain, born and bred on the Isle of the Lost, and that's where my loyalties should be. I shouldn't be worried about Ben, or his family, or the few friends I've made, or anyone else in Auradon. *Stop being so weak,* Maleficent would say. *We're about to have all the power in the kingdom. Hers and hers crowns. The ability to bend good and evil to our will. What more could a girl want?*

I never knew it before . . . but after the past week, I realize a girl *can* want a lot more than that. I'm not sure world domination was ever what I wanted, really. My mother was the one who always told me power was the most important thing. Before I could walk she was going on about storming Auradon and throwing Belle and the Beast out of the castle. She was the one who would shout, "LONG LIVE EVIL!" every morning when she woke up, or say it quietly to herself as she admired the spiderwebs in our kitchen. *They did this to me,* she told me once, after her magic failed. *They weakened my powers. They took away my strength. They sent me here to rot, but I will have my revenge.*

Where was my choice? When do I get to decide who I am and what I want to be? Why has everything always been chosen for me?

Maybe it's not worth questioning. I *have* to get the wand—I can't face my mother without it. I should just put this cupcake for Ben in a box, and save it for the day of the coronation. I'll give it to him before I steal the wand. That's the only thing I can do to help, the only choice I have now.

So I choose to set him free.

A MILLION
THOUGHTS IN
MY HEAD

SHOULD I LET
MY HEART KEEP
LISTENING?

I KNOW IT'S TIME
TO SAY GOOD-BYE

BUT IT'S SO HARD
TO LET GO

I CAN'T BELIEVE I EVER THOUGHT WE WOULD FIT IN HERE.

# I SHOULD NEVER HAVE EVEN CONSIDERED THE IDEA THAT I COULD BE ANYTHING BESIDES A VILLAIN, A BADDIE, THE EVIL MALEFICENT'S DAUGHTER.

Today, Family Day, proved that could never happen. It was a complete disaster. Carlos, Evie, Jay, and I must've spent an hour getting ready, trying to find outfits that would help us blend in as much as possible. It was already bad enough that we were the only kids in the school without anyone showing up for us. We didn't want to look like outcasts, too. Jay settled on some plain button-down shirt, and I chose a skirt like the ones all the princesses here wear. It's humiliating to think about it. We walked onto the great lawn, and there were dozens of beautiful, picture-perfect families, all smiling and laughing.

# STUDENTS HUGGING THEIR MOMS. LITTLE BROTHERS AND SISTERS PLAYING ON THE GRASS. EVERYONE SEEMED SO HAPPY.

## THINGS WERE OKAY AT FIRST. EVERYBODY WAS SO CAUGHT UP IN THEIR

mini family reunions that they hardly noticed us. Carlos and Jay chowed down on some chocolate-covered strawberries. Of course Jay was flirting with some girls from the cheer squad. It was a while before I spotted Ben and his parents. They were together taking family pictures. When Ben introduced me as his girlfriend, their mouths fell open. Belle looked like someone had just told her talking clocks and candelabra don't exist.

That actually wasn't the bad part, though—not even close. Because as much as Belle and the Beast weren't jump-up-and-down thrilled that Ben and I are dating, it only took them a few minutes to warm up to me. The Beast invited me to have lunch with them, and Belle even said my friends could come. She seemed to like the fact that I actually had friends, and that I didn't want them to have to hang around the party alone, feeling left out.

No, Belle and the Beast weren't the problem. Everything started right after that, when I was looking for Evie, Carlos, and Jay in the crowd. I bumped into this elderly queen. When she saw me, her face changed. It looked pinched, like she just got a whiff of rotten meat. *Now, have we met?* she asked, staring at me. I didn't recognize her, though I'd heard my mom's stories a hundred times before. It wasn't until Audrey came over and called her "Grammy" that I put it together.

# QUEEN LEAH.
# AS IN AURORA'S MOTHER. ALSO KNOWN AS MALEFICENT'S WORST ENEMY.

I can still see her expression, how her eyes narrowed at me. At first she thought I was my mom, that I'd somehow preserved myself for decades using some crazy fountain of youth magic. *How are you here?!* she whispered fiercely. *And how have you stayed so young?!* Then Ben jumped in to help. But as soon as he explained who I was (*Oh, this is just Mal! Maleficent's daughter!*) and that I was at Auradon Prep because of his proclamation, she started screaming.

*These children need a chance to what, Ben?! Destroy us?* she yelled. Then she turned to everyone on the great lawn, trying to get them on her side. It didn't take much. A crowd had already formed around us. They were all staring at me like I'd just transformed into a python. Chad was standing a few feet away, watching, thrilled that he finally had a reason to lash out at us in front of everyone. *They were raised by their parents, Ben,* he said. *What do you think villains teach their children?!*

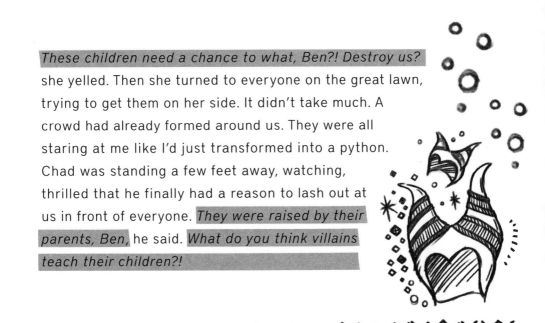

# I DON'T REALLY REMEMBER HOW IT HAPPENED. I KNOW EVIE, CARLOS,

and Jay came up behind me, and Chad was yelling at them, too, accusing them of stealing and cheating. He was telling everyone how horrible we were. People in the crowd were whispering and laughing at us. I heard someone mutter something about sending us back, how they never wanted us here in the first place. Then Evie reached for her magic mirror. Chad pushed it out of her hands. I think that's when Jay lost it—he just snapped. He and Chad started fighting and then, suddenly, Chad was on the ground. Evie had used the atomizer on him—two spritzes and he was knocked out cold.

We ran all the way back to the dorms, trying to get as far from everyone as possible. It's only been an hour, not even, since we left. I don't know what's going to happen to us now. They'll probably send Evie back to the island after what she's done. Maybe we'll all be expelled.

I know Evie was just trying to stop Chad from fighting Jay. I know she was just trying to help. And a week ago I would've loved to have seen her spray that potion right in Chad's smug little face. But something has changed . . . things are different now. *We're* different. We're not who they say we are—we're not all bad.

# I JUST WISH SOMEONE BESIDES BEN COULD SEE THAT. . . .

# So I'm still here. It's Thursday night,

four days after the incident at Family Day, and I'm still in my dorm room at Auradon Prep. I haven't been expelled. In fact, none of us have. Ben must've explained what happened to Fairy Godmother, because we just got a stern talking-to from her, some lecture about not using an atomizer at school, and counting to ten before we do anything we might regret.

Who cares, though, really. Ben only treated me so nicely because he's under a love spell, convinced that we're more alike than we are. I have to keep reminding myself that it wasn't real. Whatever happened on the date, whatever I felt, it was part of the love spell. Ben is going to be the king of Auradon. His parents are my mother's sworn enemies.

## There's no way he'd fall for me, of all girls, when he could be with someone like Audrey. They're both good. I'm evil. End of story.

Here's the thing, though: I'm done with this place. They should've expelled me when they had the chance, because after what happened in school today, I don't care about anyone here—and they definitely don't care about us.

# NO ONE HAS SPOKEN TO ANY OF US SINCE SUNDAY. I PASSED LONNIE IN THE HALL (YES, THE SAME LONNIE WHO JUST A FEW DAYS AGO WAS COMING TO MY ROOM FOR A NEW HAIRSTYLE, TELLING ME HOW COOL I AM)

and she stared at the ground, pretending she didn't see me. Whether Doug helped Evie or not, he didn't have the guts to sit with us at lunch. Ben is the only Auradon Prep student who's come within a ten-foot radius of any of us, and that's only because he's under a love spell.

## AS SOON AS I GIVE HIM THE CUPCAKE, HE'LL BE CRYING "EVIL!" WITH EVERYONE ELSE.

# To make everything worse, Audrey has used this as the perfect opportunity to turn everyone in her pretty, prissy princess clique against me.

Even Jane has been following her around like a sheep, hanging on her every word, laughing at her (completely unfunny) jokes. At lunch, Ben had barely left the picnic table area when Audrey started going on and on about how Ben doesn't actually like me, how it's just part of a "bad girl phase." Then Jane joined in, saying that he'd never make a villain queen (as if I *want* to be queen). I couldn't stop myself, though—my eyes went a deep emerald green, the way they always do when I'm angry. I muttered a spell under my breath and undid Jane's new look, turning her hair back into the dull, lifeless mess it was before.

There's no point in trying anymore. There's no point in pretending we're anything but what they think we are. Bad, rotten, evil. I was so stupid to worry about Auradon, about Ben and his family, or any of the people we've met here. Everyone sees us as our parents' children. Thieves. Liars. Manipulators. Cheats.

So they think we're villains?
Well, they ain't seen nothing yet.

## The day is finally here. All this time we've spent planning

and plotting, trying to figure out the best way to take the wand—it's all led up to this. Evie's down the hall in the dorm bathrooms, getting ready for the coronation. (She claims those mirrors have better light. If there's anyone who's an expert on reflections, it's her.) I've put on the dress she designed for me, this big puffy gown that's cool without trying too hard to be. She's already done my makeup. The window's open and I can hear the music playing on the school quad. That means the carriage has already left the carriage house. Ben is picking me up before everyone else—we're supposed to make a grand procession through the streets of Auradon. All the citizens will come out of their cottages, and Ben will wave and smile. I'll be sitting right beside him.

# I CAN'T THINK ABOUT WHAT WILL HAPPEN TO BEN AND HIS FAMILY.

But you know what? It doesn't matter. You'd think I was the one who had been under the love spell, the way I've let whatever happened between us get to me. He's only being nice to us because of the spell. I have to remember that every time he looked into my eyes and said something sweet, every time he did something nice for me, it was only because I made him do it. The proclamation was just some experiment he tried out, and after Family Day it was clear to every-one—it didn't work. He doesn't care what happens to us. Not really.

# I CAN SEE THE CARRIAGE FROM THE WINDOW—IT JUST ROUNDED THE CORNER AND IS PULLING UP THE LONG AURADON PREP DRIVEWAY. I BETTER SAY GOOD-BYE TO EVIE AND GO DOWNSTAIRS. BEN IS WAITING FOR ME.

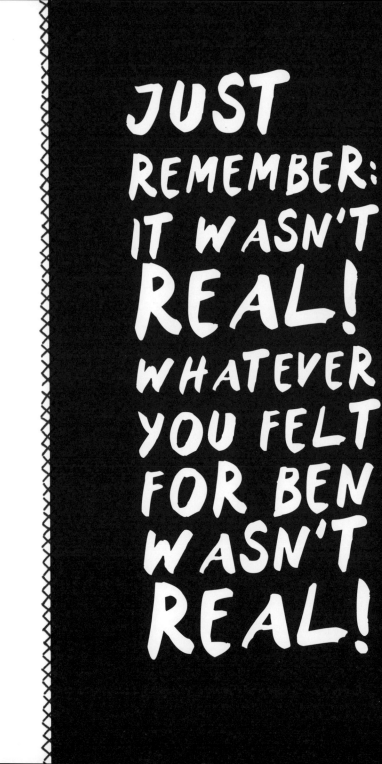

No no no no no no no no. This cannot be happening. This wasn't what was supposed to happen. This was not part of the plan. I am seriously freaking out right now.

## So I'm at the coronation, hiding in a bathroom stall.

I told Ben I just needed a few minutes to freshen up before we went into the cathedral. There are so many people here, and everyone is taking pictures of us and calling out our names. I can't think with all these people yelling: *Here! Over here! Smile for the camera! Prince Benjamin! Mal! Mal! Mal!*

°₀°o·°₀°o·°₀°o·

Okay. I need to figure out what to do. I don't even know how I feel. I went down to meet Ben in the carriage, and he looked adorable, and he was being all sweet to me, and I just kept reminding myself: it's not real, it's the love spell, don't think about it too much, you're so close to the wand, don't mess it up now! Ben could tell I was nervous, because he grabbed my hand and told me that it would be fine, that I could relax. Then he pulled off his Auradon Prep ring and asked if I would wear it. As like a symbol . . . of us.

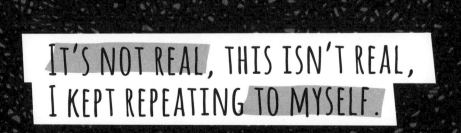

It's not real, this isn't real,
I kept repeating to myself.

## THEN I TOLD BEN THAT I COULDN'T WEAR THE RING, AT LEAST

not right now—it's too big; what if it just slipped off during the coronation? He seemed confused. Then it got more than a little awkward, so I pulled out the chocolate cupcake I made for him and gave him that, saying it was a present and he should eat it later. As a post-coronation snack.

He didn't listen. Before I could stop him, he popped the whole thing in his mouth and swallowed it in one bite. I just stared at him, waiting for him to look around and wonder why he was sitting in the carriage with me and not Audrey. I was afraid he might immediately freak out that we were holding hands. But nothing changed. When I asked him if he still had strong feelings for me, he just smiled and said, *Not sure, let's give the anti-love potion a few minutes to take effect.*

## THE ANTI-LOVE POTION. HE KNEW ABOUT THE SPELL ALL ALONG.

*It's fine*, he said. *You had a crush on me. I was with Audrey. You just didn't trust that it could happen on its own. Am I right?*

# RIGHT . . . I TOLD HIM,

## YES, SURE, THAT WAS EXACTLY WHAT HAPPENED.

Apparently the spell washed off when Ben went swimming in the enchanted lake, which was . . . a long time ago. Everything after that was real. When he stuck up for me and my friends at Family Day, even when no one else would. . . . When he sat with us every day at lunch after that. As soon as he'd gotten out of the lake, he told me he loved me.

*What about you?* he'd asked. *Do you love me?*

*I don't know what love is,* I'd said.

*Maybe I can teach you. . . .*

# WHAT AM I SUPPOSED TO DO WITH THAT?! HOW AM I SUPPOSED TO BETRAY HIM NOW? HE PUT HIS RING ON MY FINGER. I DON'T KNOW WHAT TO DO, BUT I HAVE TO FIGURE IT OUT. I HAVE TO GO BACK OUTSIDE, BACK TO THE CORONATION. BACK TO BEN.

**HE'S WAITING FOR ME.**

## So much has happened today I don't even know where to start.

I've been happy, sad, scared, hopeful, desperate, lovesick, nervous.
. . . Pretty much every emotion you could feel, I've felt, and it's not
even four o'clock. (Oh! And there was a surprise appearance from
my mother! More on that later. . . .)

Right. So. I guess I'll start where I left off, right after I found out Ben
had known about the love spell all along. After that we went into the
cathedral, and I took my seat in the front row, maybe ten feet away
from the wand. When Ben came down the aisle, all eyes were on
him. He stood in front of his parents and then Fairy Godmother did
the honors, removing the crown from the Beast's head and setting it
on Ben's. She said something about justice and mercy and reigning
with integrity . . . and then it happened. Ben knelt in front of her and
his father lifted the glass cover off the wand. Then Belle handed the
wand to Fairy Godmother. It was shimmering this perfect crystal
turquoise color.

I kept staring at it, trying to figure out the best moment to lunge
forward and grab it. There were a few times it seemed possible, but
Jane was standing right next to me, blocking my way. When Fairy
Godmother was in front of Ben, the wand just above his shoulder, I
knew I finally had my chance. This was what we came to Auradon to
do—CARLOS, EVIE, AND JAY WERE ALL COUNTING ON ME.

I DIDN'T THINK ABOUT BEN IN THAT MOMENT, OR WORRY HOW BETRAYED HE MIGHT FEEL. I GUESS THAT'S THE HARD THING NOW, AFTER THE FACT. I WAS ONLY THINKING ABOUT MYSELF. MY MOM'S WORDS KEPT RINGING IN MY EARS: DON'T BE WEAK, MAL. IT'S WEAK TO CARE ABOUT PEOPLE. I JUST WANTED THE WAND, I WANTED TO GRAB IT, TO HAVE IT IN MY HANDS . . . TO FINALLY WIN.

. . . . . . . . . . . . . . . . . . . . . . . . . . . . .

I stepped forward, my eyes locked on the wand. Fairy Godmother started saying something about blessing Ben, and does he solemnly swear something, she now pronounces him . . . I could barely hear her. I was too focused on taking another step, then another, closing in on our prize. I was just a few feet away when someone pushed in front of me. It happened so fast it took me a second to realize it was Jane. She yanked the wand out of her mother's hand.

. . . . . . . . . . . . . . . . . . . . . . . . . . . . .

We all just stared at her as she tried to control the wand. It glittered and sparked. A lightning bolt shot out the end of it, breaking one of the cathedral windows and splitting up into the sky. *If you won't make me beautiful, I'll do it myself!* Jane yelled. Bibbidi-Bobbidi-Boo . . .

. . . . . . . . . . . . . . . . . . . . . . . . . . . . .

I HAD TO PINCH MYSELF TO MAKE SURE IT WAS REAL. I COULDN'T BELIEVE WHAT I WAS WATCHING. JANE HAD HER GRIMY LITTLE HANDS ON THE WAND—MY WAND—THE ONE I'D BEEN PLOTTING TO STEAL FOR WEEKS. I WANTED IT FOR ULTIMATE POWER, WORLD DOMINATION, AND FREEDOM FROM THE ISLE OF THE LOST. AND ALL SHE WANTED WAS A SILLY MAKEOVER.

She couldn't even hold it up right. Sparks were flying everywhere. As soon as she turned her back to me, I charged her. Every inch of me was alive as I aimed the wand at Fairy Godmother, then the rest of the crowd, ordering them to stay back. Carlos, Evie, and Jay all rushed to my side.

Let's go, Carlos said, grabbing my arm.

Revenge time, Jay whispered.

# IF ONLY I HADN'T LOOKED AT BEN. HIS FACE WAS PALE.

He had this expression that I'd never seen on him before. He seemed so . . . disappointed. **I had to remind myself that he doesn't understand what it's like to grow up the child of a villain.** He's never met my mom or heard how she talks to me. Ever since Ben was a kid his parents have been kind, loving, and supportive. They've taught him to be good. No matter how much I care about him, how could he ever know what it's like to be me? It was easy for him to say, "Choose good." He never had to.

# UGH. It's hard to think about it all right now, after the fact. It's almost like . . . *embarrassing* . . . the way I acted. Anyway. There's more of the story to tell, but the coronation after-party has already started out on the school quad. They're playing the music pretty loud. Evie just peeked her head in our room and waved for me to go.

# I SHOULD GO. IT'S TIME TO GET THE PARTY STARTED! MORE LATER . . .

# LAST NIGHT WAS AMAZING. TOTALLY AWESOME, COOL, FUN, GREAT . . . ALL THE ADJECTIVES I NEVER WOULD'VE USED A FEW MONTHS AGO.

We danced all night at the party, me with Ben, Jay with the whole cheer squad (apparently they LOVE bad boys), and Carlos with Dude. I even caught Evie dancing with Doug every now and then. All of Auradon Prep was lit up with different neon lights and everyone was just having a good time.

## IT WAS GOOD. NOW I LIKE THAT WORD.

Okay, where did I leave off? . . . The wand. Right. I had it in my hands, and we were about to leave, when I looked at Ben.

*Your parents made their choices*, he said. *Now you make yours.*

Those words . . . as soon as he said them, I could feel a lump rising in the back of my throat. I had to blink back tears. I wanted to run away with my friends, but I couldn't. I just stood there, staring at him, as he went on. He told me he knew I was good inside. He's always known, and when I asked him how, he said he was listening to his heart. . . .

**That's what really got me.** Because the truth is, I'd only been at Auradon Prep a few days when I started to hear it—what I really thought, felt, and wanted. It was like all the things my mother said weren't as important when she wasn't right there, demanding I listen to her. I started to hear my heart, just a whisper at first, telling me that Ben was kind. It was what made me laugh when Lonnie was hanging out with us in our room—our first real friend at Auradon.

# AND I HEARD IT LOUDER THAN EVER WHEN BEN WAS LOOKING AT ME WITH HIS SWEET, KIND EYES AND TELLING ME HE LOVED ME.

I WANTED TO
LISTEN TO

LOVE AND MAGIC, MAL x

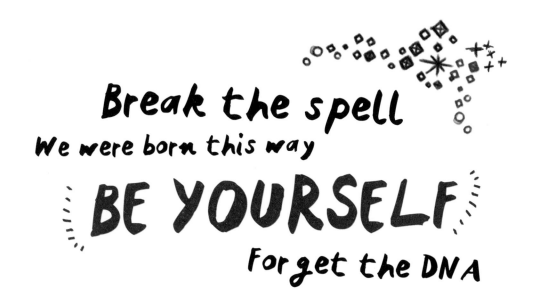

Break the spell
We were born this way
BE YOURSELF
Forget the DNA

Start a chain reaction
Never let it stop
LET'S SET IT OFF

# Kings and Queens

It's our time to RISE

## Write the book

# THE STORY OF OUR LIVES

# Goodness is like a castle. It requires:

Constant vigilance

A bright flag, to let the world see who you are

A place to watch out for trouble

Space enough inside for all those who seek the shelter of your friendship

Plenty of windows through which to let the light of knowledge in

A strong door, through which only good may enter

A firm foundation, without which goodness may crumble

I gotta go, though—I'm supposed to meet Ben outside on the quad for a ride on his scooter. I'm his date, his really real date, who he's actually with (real love, not fake love . . . did I mention that?!). For the first time in a long time, I feel this really weird feeling. It's all over, and sometimes it makes me feel like I'm floating, and other times I just get a sudden case of the smiles.

# I'M HAPPY.
# REALLY, TRULY HAPPY.

(Okay . . . going for real now. Seriously. We're trying to catch the sunset. ☺)

...D I FORGOT TO MENTION WHAT HAPPENED TO JANE.

Fairy Godmother was obviously pretty upset with her. She was lecturing her about her stunt with the wand when I stepped in. I had to defend her—I knew that it was my fault. I was the one who had put all those ideas in her head about needing a makeover and not being pretty enough. If I hadn't talked to her that day in the bathroom, she never would've done that. I still kind of feel bad about it, that I would ever make her feel like she was ugly. (What an ugly thought . . .)

Just doing that small thing, though—taking responsibility for what I said to Jane—made me feel better. I can see it now, how all the little choices I've made have amounted to something. Every time I choose to do better, I feel better. It's kind of . . . cool.

# IS THAT CHEESY?
## WHO CARES.

And Ben . . . I keep going back to this one moment. As soon as Fairy Godmother unfroze the crowd, Ben ran forward, ready to defend me. He let out a beastly roar. It took him a few seconds to realize my mother wasn't in the cathedral anymore. He looked down at the newt and laughed. *Next time I rescue you, okay?* he said, pulling me into a hug.

# IT FELT SO GOOD TO BE IN HIS ARMS. I LET HIM HOLD ME THERE FOR A LITTLE WHILE, EVEN IF EVERYONE WAS WATCHING.

# I JUST GOT BACK FROM MY FIRST DAY AT AURADON PREP.

I know, I know, technically I've been here longer, but this felt like my first day. When Evie, Jay, Carlos, and I were walking down the hall, everyone was looking at us differently.

INSTEAD OF BEING THE OUTCASTS FROM THE ISLE OF THE LOST WHO NO ONE CAN REALLY TRUST, WE WERE THE KIDS WHO CHANGED EVERYTHING AT THE CORONATION. THE ONES WHO PROVED BEN WAS RIGHT—THAT WE DID DESERVE A SECOND CHANCE.

· · · · · · · · · · · · · · · ·

I KEPT REPEATING THOSE WORDS. AT FIRST I DIDN'T THINK THE
spell was working. The dragon just stared me down. It wasn't until
the fourth time I said it that my mother's eyes widened. She blinked
once and then—**poof!**—she disappeared in a cloud of smoke.

I didn't know what happened. Evie wasn't sure if the spell had done
it, or what. Carlos was the one who noticed the tiny newt on the floor.

# SHE'D SHRUNK DOWN TO NOTHING.

\* \* \* \* \* \* \* \* \* \* \* \* \* \* \* \* \* \* \* \* \* \* \* \* \* \* \* \*

As I'm writing this, it's weird . . . I know I should be happy I defeated
my mother, but seeing her like that wasn't easy for me. She was so
small and helpless. This person I'd worshipped my entire life was no
bigger than my finger. Eventually Fairy Godmother was freed from her
spell, and an attendant put the glass bell jar over my mom, trapping
her inside. She's still somewhere in Auradon—Fairy Godmother is
keeping watch until we figure out what to do next.

That's not the easiest part to write about . . . or think about . . . or
remember. But I've run that moment through my head so many times,
and if I didn't stop my mother, she might've hurt someone—Jay, Evie,
or even me. I guess even if you do the right thing, there'll always be
some hard choices—nothing's ever that simple, right?

THE STRENGTH OF EVIL IS AS *
GOOD AS NONE,
I SAID, FEELING MY
FRIENDS COMING
UP BEHIND ME. *
WHEN STANDS *
BEFORE FOUR *
HEARTS AS ONE.

*The strength of evil is as good as none,* I said, feeling my friends coming up behind me. *When stands before four hearts as one.*

//////////////////////////////////////////////////////////////////////////////////

The strength of evil
IS AS GOOD AS NONE.
When stands before
FOUR HEARTS AS ONE.

THE STRENGTH OF EVIL
IS AS GOOD AS
NONE.
WHEN STANDS BEFORE
FOUR HEARTS
AS ONE.

The strength of evil
IS AS GOOD AS
NONE.
When stands before
FOUR HEARTS
AS ONE.

THE STRENGTH OF EVIL
IS AS GOOD AS NONE.
WHEN STANDS BEFORE
FOUR HEARTS AS ONE.

I didn't recognize my mother anymore. The monster that stood before me was nearly two stories tall, with fangs that hung over her bottom lip and nostrils that flared when she breathed. She leaned down, her eyes glowing green as she exhaled. I didn't show any fear.

I kept my eyes locked on hers, knowing that I'd have to make up my own spell if I was going to defeat her.

I recited one of the few spells I knew off the top of my head, drawing the wand to me. I didn't really expect it to work against her power, but it did. Then she did something I'd never seen before . . . she transformed.

I always knew my mother was powerful, but I never knew *how* powerful until that moment. Dark purplish-black wings sprung out from her shoulder blades. Her face grew longer, her teeth sharper as she disappeared into a cloud of green mist. When she reappeared, she was a fierce dragon.

# ONLY CARLOS, EVIE, JAY, AND I WERE LEFT.

My mother grabbed the wand from Fairy Godmother's hand. As soon as she held it, it sparked and shook in protest, like it was disturbed by her very presence. My mom was furious that I'd tried to stop her plan. She made some comment about me not being evil enough to be her, about how I didn't have enough practice and talent to command power the way she did. Then she noticed Ben's ring on my finger and told me there was no room for love in my life.

# THAT'S WHEN I SNAPPED.
I COULDN'T JUST STAND THERE, LISTENING TO HER TELL ME ABOUT MY LIFE. WHAT DID SHE KNOW ABOUT WHO I WAS AND WHAT I WANTED? HOW COULD SHE SAY I DIDN'T DESERVE TO BE LOVED? HOW CRUEL AND WICKED AND . . . EVIL . . . IS THAT?!

I was looking at Evie, smiling, when I heard the window break somewhere behind me. I turned, looking up at my mother as she descended into the cathedral in her glowing green ball. There was a roll of thunder and a flash of lightning. Her eyes were bright. She stared down at the wand in my hand, a wicked smile on her face as she pointed her scepter out into the crowd.

I've never seen my mother like that. SO FULL OF EVIL. The glowing green orb around her, spinning magic, feeding her strength. I've NEVER been as afraid of her as I was then.

I thought the spell had trapped her on the Isle of the Lost. I thought she couldn't reach us here. But something must've happened when Jane took the wand from Fairy Godmother. The spell must've broken.

I lunged forward, passing the wand back to Fairy Godmother. I didn't think I'd have the strength to fight my mother—not while she was like this, with all her strength restored. Fairy Godmother raised the wand to strike, but it was too late. My mom pointed her scepter into the crowd and froze everyone, including Fairy Godmother, in ice.

# I TOLD EVIE, CARLOS, AND JAY THAT. I SAID IT RIGHT THERE, IN FRONT OF EVERYONE IN THE CATHEDRAL.

I could see that my friends didn't want to ruin Auradon, either. Why would we go back to the Isle of the Lost? So Jay could go back to stealing? So Carlos could be afraid again? So Evie could go back to pretending she wasn't smart, like her mother wanted, just so she could marry a prince?

**None of us wanted that.** Ben was right—we wanted to be good, because we knew in our hearts we already were. We always have been. It doesn't matter who our parents are.

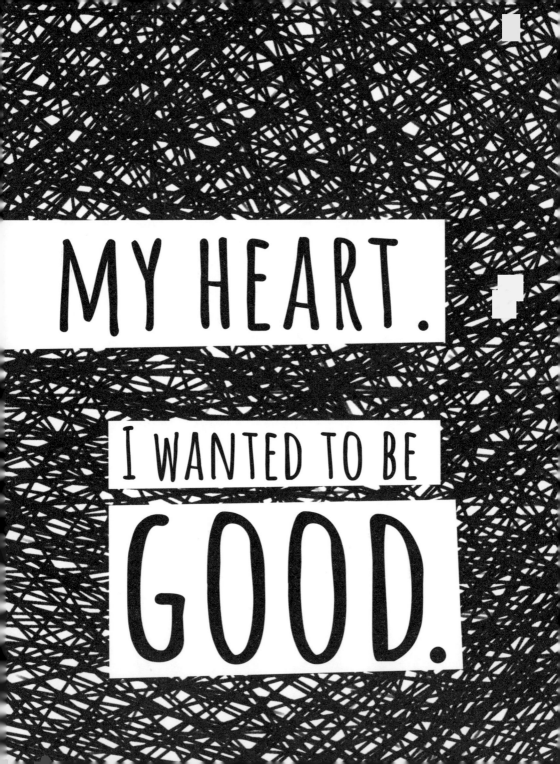